HOW TO DRAW

BUILDINGS

Pam Beasant

Designed by Iain Ashman

Edited by Judy Tatchell

Illustrated by
Iain Ashman, Isobel Gardner,
Chris Lyon and Chris Smedley

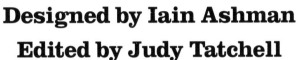

Contents

Consultant: Iain Ashman
Consultant architect: Peter Reed

About this book

There are all sorts of exciting buildings for you to draw in this book, ranging from a cathedral to a space station. Clear, step-by-step instructions show you how to build up your pictures in stages.

Basic drawing and colouring skills and styles are introduced with many professional hints and techniques.

For instance, you can find out about perspective on page 7 and composition on page 18. Throughout the book there are tips on how to add convincing details such as shadows and highlights.

On pages 26-27, you can learn the basics of technical drawing and how to plan, draw and build your own model house.

There is a round-up of techniques and drawing tools (such as pencils and paints) on pages 30-31, to help you choose your equipment.

Drawing styles

The drawings in this book are done in various styles. Some of the main ones are shown here.

Pen and ink

Ink colour washes (see ▶ below) are added over line drawings to create shadows, highlights and graded areas of colour.

Try this pen and ink haunted house on pages 10-11.

Once you build up confidence, you can have fun experimenting with any style you choose.

Line drawings

◀ Line drawings are done with pen or pencil. You use lines or dots to give an impression of shadow. You can find out more about line drawing technique on page 15.

Washes

A wash is a thin coat of watery paint or ink. It gives a subtle, overall colour to a drawing. You can add more layers for areas of stronger colour or shadow. You can also mix and blend different coloured washes on the same drawing. (Before using a wash, see page 31 for how to stretch paper.)

Line drawing.

First layer of wash.

There is a comic book style future city on pages 20-21.

"Impressionism"

A looser style, giving an atmospheric impression of a scene, can be achieved by blending soft lines and colours.
▼

Find out more about this style on pages 24-25.

Comic book style ▲

Comic book style uses bold, black lines and deep colours. It is dramatic and can have a lot of movement.

Airbrush

◄ The smooth, flat, airbrush style is often used for modern or futuristic subjects such as skyscrapers or space cities.

There are skyscrapers to draw on pages 16-17.

Cartoons

◄ A cartoon style can add character and a sense of fun to a drawing. It exaggerates and changes some aspects of the subject to make it funny.

There is a cartoon castle to draw on page 8.

Darker colour for shadow.

Finished picture.

The first layer of wash should be very weak and watery. Then add more paint to the wash mixture to make it a darker, more concentrated shade. Apply each further layer when the last is dry. In this way, you can gradually build up contrasting areas of light and dark.

For most of the drawings in this book, you can use any colouring tools you choose, such as felt tips. You need not stick to the tools and techniques used by this book's illustrators if you do not want to.

3

Looking at buildings

It is a good idea to carry a small sketchbook with you when you go out for a walk. You can make quick sketches of any interesting buildings or details that you see. You can use these sketches later to invent your own drawings of buildings. You could use photographs instead, although sketching helps you to see how buildings are put together.

Windows and doors

Try sketching a variety of windows and doors on one page. This is a good way to compare and contrast details and experiment with sketching.

Fit as many details as you can on to one page.

How buildings fit together

Sketching real buildings is the best way to see how they fit together, and how their details vary. You could try a street or a row of shop-fronts.

Note how the shades are paler, the further away the buildings are.

You can concentrate on one building in a scene. Draw just the shadowy outline of the others to frame it.

A quick, loose sketch.

You can write small notes on your sketch about colour, detail and texture.

A tight, finished sketch.

Sketching a near skyline is good practice for perspective drawing.

Painting your sketches

If you take a small paintbox and a sealed water container on your sketching trip, you can paint your drawing immediately. This is a good way to practise showing realistic light and shade, and mixing lifelike colours.

Overlap colours to emphasize shadows or darker areas.

Dab wet paint with a tissue for a textured look.

Skylines

A skyline is often needed for background in a drawing, or to give it depth. Sketching one is a good way to see the overall shape of a city.

Period styles

Every age has had a different general building style. These vary around the world. There are some examples below.

Ancient Egyptian (2600-30BC)

Classical Greek (600BC)

Islamic (700-1200)

Romanesque (1100-1200)

Gothic (1200-1400)

Byzantine (1600-1700)

Baroque (1700-1800)

Neo-Classical (1800-1900)

Neo-Gothic (late 1800s)

Modern (1900-)

Castles

Castles are huge, interesting buildings with long histories. They were built by powerful people such as kings and barons. They were used as a defence against raiding enemies as well as homes. This is why their walls are so thick and high.

Castles are not as hard to draw as they look. Find out below how to draw the castle shown on these two pages.

Distant mountains should be sketchy, small and not so heavily coloured as the castle.

Drawing the castle

Draw the basic block shapes of the castle walls, as shown here.

Now add the shapes of the towers, rubbing out any unwanted lines.

Add the roofs, turrets and windows, shown in blue.

Add the drawbridge, staircase and roof flags. Sketch the stonework detail.

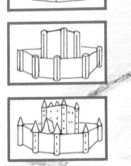

The detail on the side walls can be sketchy and pale.

The drawbridge is halfway down. Draw the angles carefully.

Different kinds of castles

There are lots of different styles of castles. The main picture shows a 14th century castle.

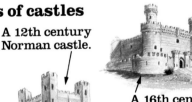

A 12th century Norman castle.

A 16th century Spanish castle.

A Gothic-style 19th century German castle. (A real-life fairytale castle.)

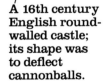

A 16th century English round-walled castle; its shape was to deflect cannonballs.

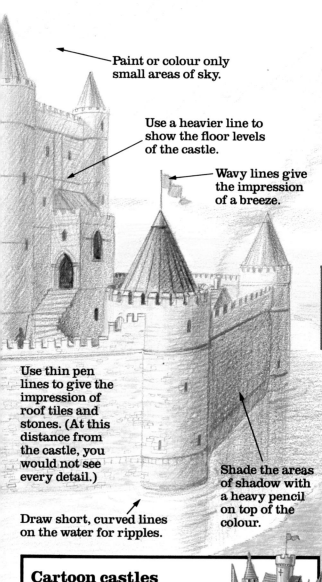

Paint or colour only small areas of sky.

Use a heavier line to show the floor levels of the castle.

Wavy lines give the impression of a breeze.

Use thin pen lines to give the impression of roof tiles and stones. (At this distance from the castle, you would not see every detail.)

Shade the areas of shadow with a heavy pencil on top of the colour.

Draw short, curved lines on the water for ripples.

Cartoon castles

Cartoon castles often have a narrow base, and the towers, turrets and flags are exaggerated. Sometimes they teeter on tall, narrow rocks. There is a fairytale castle to draw on page 8.

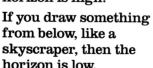

Perspective

Drawing things "in perspective" means drawing them the way your eyes see them. Perspective is based on the idea that things look smaller the further away they are. Pictures in perspective look real and three-dimensional (3-D), rather than flat.

When you look down a street with equal-sized buildings, the ones nearest look much bigger than those at the other end.

Vanishing point

On a long street, the buildings seem to get closer together until they "meet". This imaginary meeting point is the "vanishing point".

There is often more than one vanishing point on the same picture. Lines that are parallel* to each other meet at the same vanishing point.

The vanishing points are on the horizon, an imaginary eye-level line.

Horizon

If you draw something from above, then the horizon is high.

If you draw something from below, like a skyscraper, then the horizon is low.

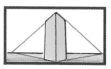

If you draw something looking straight at it, then the horizon can go through the middle.

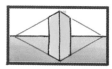

*Parallel lines are the same distance apart, like railway lines.

Fantasy buildings

Fantasy buildings are fun to invent and draw. The more detail you think of, the more convincing your fantasy world will be. Odd colours and strange figures and trees, for instance, can add life and atmosphere to your pictures. The ideas and techniques on these pages might help start you off.

Cartoons

Cartoons are not as easy as they look, because they are not strict copies of real things. Artists can use them to make jokes or comments (in newspaper cartoons, for instance) or to express imaginative ideas. Many of the buildings on these two pages are cartoons.

Professional cartoonists often draw quickly, using bold, incomplete lines. Try drawing a cartoon of your own house. Sketch the main shape loosely. Do not worry about getting lines too straight or filling in exact details.

Fairytale castle

In this drawing of a fairytale castle, lots of realistic details are either exaggerated or missed out altogether. There are lots of turrets, for instance, but no stonework or tiles on the roof.

The colours are unrealistic, with lots of pinks and purples. This helps to make the castle look magical.

Compare this drawing with the castle on the previous two pages. Try pin-pointing the things that make this one a fairytale castle.

Alien's house

This strange house belongs to an alien from a far-off planet. (There is more about imaginary space houses on page 21).

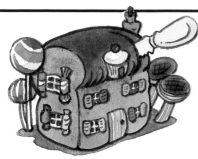

Fantasy ideas

This house is made out of different kinds of food. The main shape is easy to draw, but the details may take some time.

These cloud-people live in strange, fluffy cloud-houses. A huge umbrella over the top keeps the rain off.

This elves' workshop is full of machines and contraptions. You could use pale colours over a dark wash for the firelight.

Underwater city

This mysterious underwater city has been abandoned by its inhabitants. All sorts of sea creatures live here and the buildings are overgrown with seaweed.

Draw the far buildings very faintly, as if seen through murky water.

If you want your space house to look impressive, use a realistic style and paint or colour the picture very smoothly. Try to use muted or metallic colours.

For this picture, draw the nearest buildings first. Strong shadows and highlights and odd skies will help make your picture exciting and different.

Draw broken pillars, bits of statue lying on their sides and crumbling stairs.

Dark streaks for seaweed will give the impression of being underwater.

Haunted house

An old, dark house can be made to look haunted and very creepy, and is great fun to draw. Ramshackle walls and roofs with slates missing make it look abandoned and mysterious. Oddly-shaped shadows, strange lights behind windows and big, dark trees all give your picture lots of spooky atmosphere.

Moonlight suggests witches and werewolves, and casts interesting light and shadow on the house (see opposite).

Graded amounts of white or black added to blue paint makes shades ranging from pale to deep blue. You can use these on different parts of the drawing.

Dramatic perspective

The perspective of this haunted house makes it look huge and terrifying. It is drawn as if you are looking from ground level, so the base looks wider than the top. (See page 7 for more about perspective.)

It is a bit more difficult to draw a house in this perspective, but it is worth trying, as your drawing will look very dramatic.

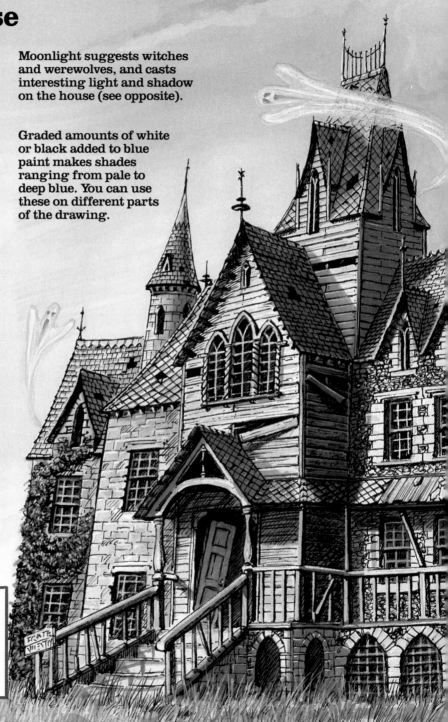

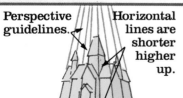

Perspective guidelines.

Horizontal lines are shorter higher up.

White streaks of paint for lightning will add atmosphere to your picture.

A strange light at a window will give the impression of a ghost. Fill half the window with shadow, in a vaguely human shape.

Look at the details on the roof and round the doors and windows. They all help to add a sinister feeling.

Large, dead trees beside the house look menacing. Make the branches thin and spiky, like fingers reaching out.

How to draw the house

First draw the basic shape of the house. Make sure that you have left enough space for windows and doors.

Add the turrets and the jutting sections of roof. Draw the lines straight at first. You can use them as guidelines to produce a more tumbledown look at a later stage.

Now draw the steps and the balcony at the front of the house.

Draw close lines across the roof for slates. When you colour the roof in, leave some black holes to show that some slates are missing.

Draw the wooden planks, leaving out a few. Draw the loose ones last, hanging down over the others.

Light and shadow

The light and shadow in your picture are important as they create atmosphere. Moonlight will make part of the house light, while the rest will be in deep shadow. This suggests that things are lurking there.

Drawing shadows

Shadows always fall away from the source of light, the sun or the moon. So all the shadows in one picture should go in the same direction.

Something that is directly below the light has a short, squashed shadow.

Something standing at an angle to the light source will have a longer, more stretched shadow.

Ruins

Ruins can look ghostly and menacing, or sad and lonely. They make imaginative drawings but they can be quite difficult as they do not have a regular shape. The step-by-step instructions below show you how to make exciting, convincing drawings of ruins.

A ruined church

This pencil drawing has a soft, atmospheric look. Varying the strength of line and shade can give the drawing texture and a feeling of depth.

Buildings usually crumble at the top first, and particularly around any door and window openings.

Draw the original shape of the window as a guide, then draw the ruined shape.

This way of shading, using lots of thin, criss-cross lines, is called cross-hatching.

Drawing the church

1. First, draw the original shape of the church faintly, to act as a guide. The lines can be rubbed out later.

2. Using a heavier line, draw the ruined shape of the church. (Rub out the first lines.)

3. Now draw the arches of the church and add details such as the windows and doors.

Adding atmosphere

Stormy skies and menacing trees add atmosphere to your drawing.

Old, crumbling graves make the church look even more abandoned.

Draw bits of fallen and broken stone and brick on the ground.

A bird perched on the window frame, or bushes growing in the doorway, make the church look deserted.

Draw the stones with a slightly wavering line, as if the edges have crumbled off. Add small black dots for moss.

A ruined street

After a disaster, such as an earthquake or a war, whole towns or cities can become almost complete ruins. The street below has suffered a great deal of damage and the houses have all been abandoned.

Draw large, black, scorched patches on the walls and round the windows.

You could draw some furniture inside the houses. Use your own furniture as a guide.

Draw pictures and torn wallpaper on some walls, and roof rafters and rubble on the floors.

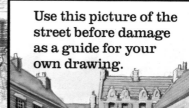

Use this picture of the street before damage as a guide for your own drawing.

You can sketch windows, doors and any interesting details on houses near you, and use them in your picture.

How to draw the street

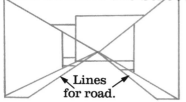

Lines for road.

Draw two lines for the road. This will act as a guide when drawing the buildings in perspective (see page 7).

Draw the houses nearest to you first. Lightly sketch the original shapes as a guide before drawing the ruined shape.

Draw the internal walls and other details, working down the street. There will be heaps of debris lying about.

13

Ancient buildings

Temples or churches are often the most important and elaborate buildings in a civilization. You can find out on these pages how to draw four examples from around the world. The buildings date from around 1500BC to the Middle Ages.

Egyptian temple

The figures on the walls need not be too accurate, as the picture is not a close-up.

Temples like this were ▶ built for many centuries when the Egyptians had a huge empire. The walls are covered with pictures of gods and goddesses.

1. Draw the main shape of the temple. Note that all walls slope inwards.

2. Now add the raised roof, the front towers, the gateway and the flagpoles.

3. Draw the columns and the wall pictures to complete the temple.

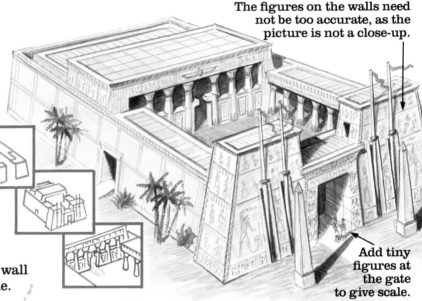

Add tiny figures at the gate to give scale.

Mayan temple

◀ This 5th century pyramid-temple was built by the Maya people of Guatemala. Its ruins are still at the site of the Lost City of Rio Azul.

Incense was burned during sacred rituals, such as burials.

1. Draw the pyramid shape. Roughly plot then draw the cross-lines and steps.

2. Rub out the pyramid peak. Draw the top building in blocks.

3. Add the stairway and sketch in the wall paintings.

Gothic cathedral

Gothic cathedrals like this were built ▶ all over medieval Europe. The high, thin walls and turrets were richly carved.

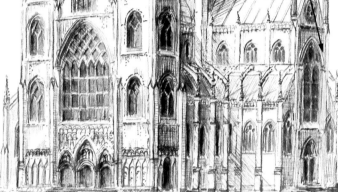

A lighter touch on the far side gives an impression of size and distance.

1. Draw the blocks which make up the main shape of the building.*

2. Draw the roofs and turrets. Start at the front and work back.

3. Add the doors and windows. Then start to add the detail of the carved stonework.

Greek temple

Temples like the one in this picture were built in Greece around the 5th century BC. The style has been copied in Europe right up to the present day.

▼

1. Draw the main, rectangular shape. Be careful about the perspective.

2. Now draw the roof shape and mark in the tops and bottoms of columns.

3. Complete the columns and add the carved details on the front end of the building.

If you draw upright lines in perspective (see page 7), a building may look as if it is leaning backwards. Architectural illustrators tend to draw upright lines almost vertical unless they want to create the effect of extreme height or scale. 15

Skyscrapers and skylines

Skyscrapers are the tallest buildings in the world and they can make very dramatic pictures. They are quite easy shapes to draw but the perspective (see page 7) can be more difficult because they are so big.

A super-hero's view

This is the way a city would look to a super-hero swooping in to save people from disaster. Skyscrapers loom everywhere and the skyline in the distance is dominated by them.

All the pictures on these pages were airbrushed (see opposite).

1. Start by drawing straight lines as a perspective guide for the skyscrapers. They should be slightly closer together at the bottom.

2. Now draw the roofs and sides of the buildings. Keep opposite sides parallel. Try to picture how the street runs below.

3. Sketch in each floor of the skyscrapers. The lines appear to get closer together as you look down the buildings.

4. Work out where shadows will fall on the buildings and shade these areas. The shadows should be quite dark for an evening scene.

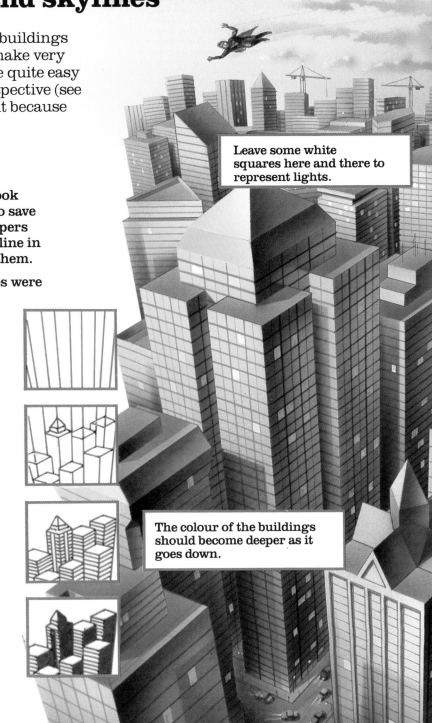

Leave some white squares here and there to represent lights.

The colour of the buildings should become deeper as it goes down.

16

A different perspective

Drawing a skyscraper from below – a worm's eye view (see page 7) – makes it look very dramatic.

This time, you have to draw the base very wide. The sides taper up to a thin, dizzy tip high above.

1. Tiny people show the building's height. Draw the floors closer as they go up.

2. White streaks on pale blue walls highlight the building and make it look glassy.

3. Other buildings reflected on the wall heighten the glassy look and add interest.

Drawing the skyline

Here the skyline shows the dark outlines of the buildings. This is called a silhouette.

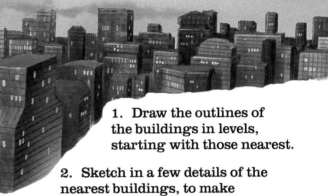

1. Draw the outlines of the buildings in levels, starting with those nearest.

2. Sketch in a few details of the nearest buildings, to make them less of a flat shape.

3. Colour everything in dark, muted colours. Watery paint produces the best effect.

Airbrushing

Many professional artists use an airbrush to produce a smooth, even finish to a picture.

The airbrush is connected to a compressed air supply which sprays a mixture of air and paint on to the drawing. Any part the artist does not want to colour is covered with a clear plastic called "masking film".

Airbrushing equipment is expensive.* You can achieve similar results if you apply felt tips or paints smoothly.

*See page 30 for more about cheaper airbrushes.

Airport

This page shows you how to plan and draw your own exciting, aerial-view picture of an airport. It is not as hard as it looks if you build up the picture in stages.

Composition

What artists decide to show in a drawing, and from which angle, is called the composition. For this airport scene, they might do several sketches from different angles to see which looks best. They could work from aerial photographs, or plans.

Plans and rough sketches.

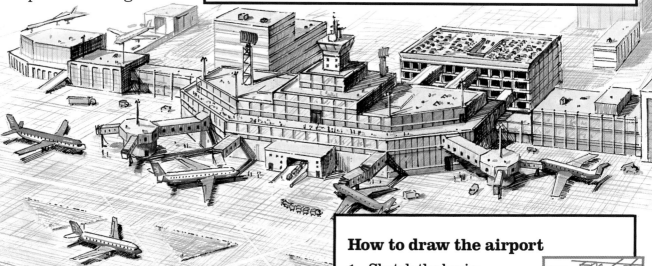

Emphasize flatness and distance by cross-hatching* runways and grass in perspective, as in this picture.

Draw long, bold, "whoosh" lines behind the plane taking off.

How to draw the airport

1. Sketch the basic shapes. You could make a perspective grid as a guide (see page 28).

2. Now draw the true shapes of the buildings. Add details such as the tower and windows.

3. Add the planes (see opposite) to bring the picture to life. Now add shadows and highlights.

*See page 12.

Railway station

This drawing of a 19th century railway station is quite hard to do, but if you work out the perspective accurately, your picture should be convincing. A pair of compasses will help you draw the roof arches.

> You can leave the roof detail quite sketchy.

> Smudge pen lines above the train with water for a smoky effect.

Small, sketchy figures give scale to the drawing.

There is a selection of trains you can draw below.

How to draw the station

First, draw perspective lines for the platform and the walls. They all go to a central vanishing point*.

Use compasses for the roof arches. Keeping the point in the same place, make each arc wider than the last.

Draw the trains, the wall detail and the benches. Add shadows and glassy highlights to the roof (see page 21).

Drawing trains and planes

These pictures might help you when drawing trains and planes. See page 23 for how to copy and enlarge the drawings using a grid.

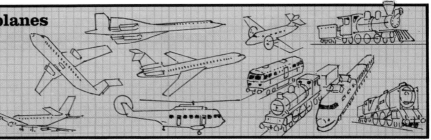

---

* See page 7.

Future cities

The future cities here are drawn in a comic book style, which uses bold, black line and large areas of flat colour. Dramatic shadows and highlights make this style atmospheric and lively. It is especially good for drawing futuristic scenes.

Space colony

This space colony is built under domes to protect people from an airless environment and from unbroken sunlight and heat.

Strong shadows along the dome's edge help to make it look 3-D.

Earth city of the future

In this future city, the huge population is housed in vast structures. Tiny trees and the traditional church show the scale of the new buildings. The picture below is divided into sections to show you how an artist might plan and draw this scene in comic book style.

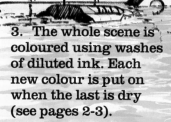

1. The artist plans the scene in pencil, checking composition* and perspective. A few door and window details are added.

2. Now everything is drawn over in waterproof ink. Finer details and shadows are added. Rough pencil lines are rubbed out.

3. The whole scene is coloured using washes of diluted ink. Each new colour is put on when the last is dry (see pages 2-3).

Bold white highlights on the domes makes them look as if they are under fierce light (see below).

The whole picture is tilted slightly to make it look dramatic and odd.

The light and shadow contrast strongly to make the scene look brightly lit.

The city details should be tiny, to give a sense of the size of the domes.

Even in the far future, some old buildings, such as this church, may be left intact.

4. The artist now highlights sunlit areas and adds shine to some buildings to make them look glassy. "Movement" lines are painted on the water and behind the small jet, above left.

Reflections and highlights

Artists use lots of different ways to highlight areas of their drawings. Some of them are shown below.

Unpainted white areas are planned at the drawing stage.

Streaks of white pencil can give a gentle, glassy sheen.

Lines of white paint produce a bold shine (see the domes above).

Black ink can show ripples and reflections in water and glass.

Space station

This is how a space station might look in the far distant future. Inside, there are huge living areas, vast hothouses and laboratories for space experiments. Solar panels provide power and there are busy docking areas for spaceships.

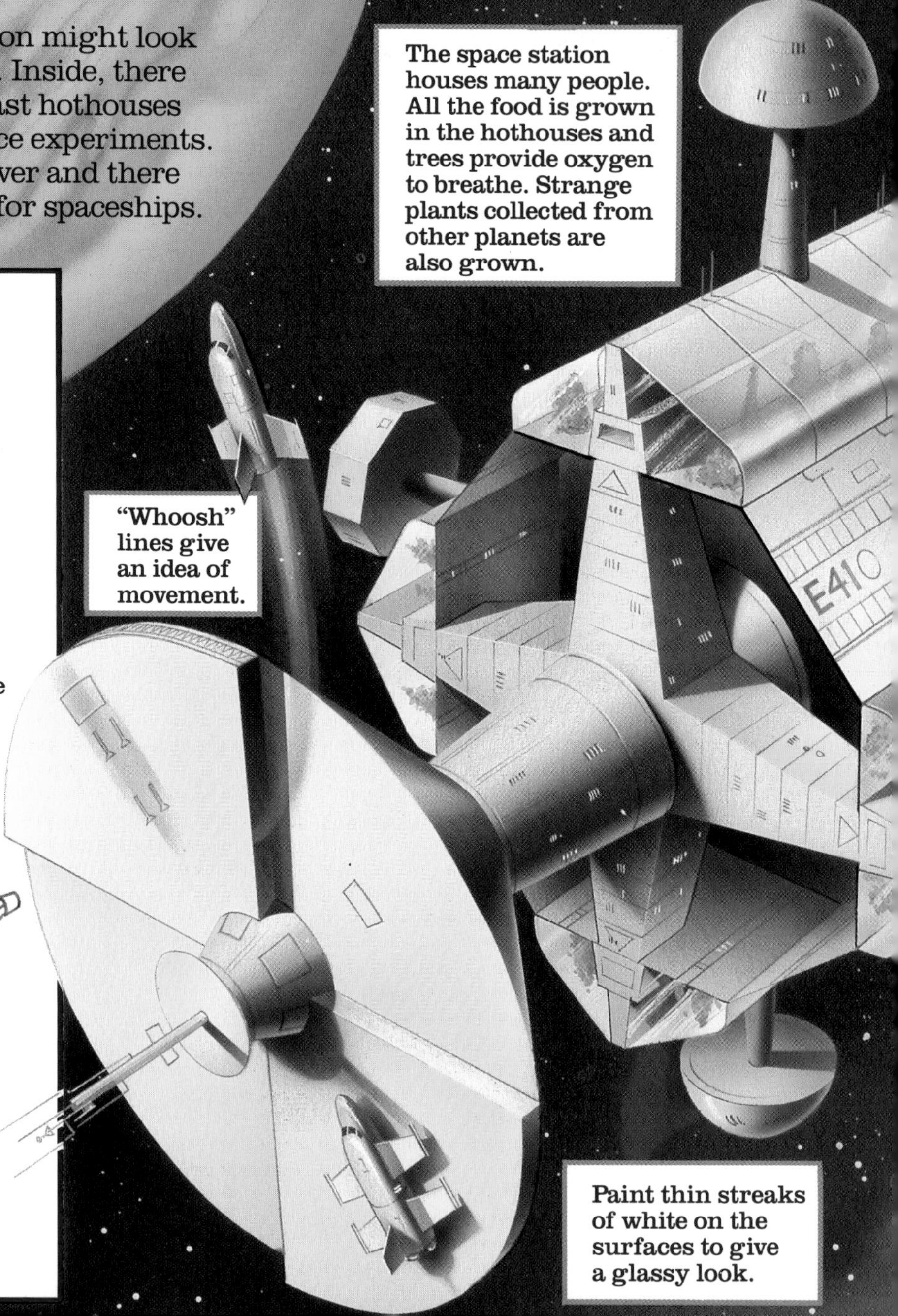

The space station houses many people. All the food is grown in the hothouses and trees provide oxygen to breathe. Strange plants collected from other planets are also grown.

Drawing the space station

The space station can be broken down into four main shapes: the central rod, an ellipse, a block and a pyramid for the nose.

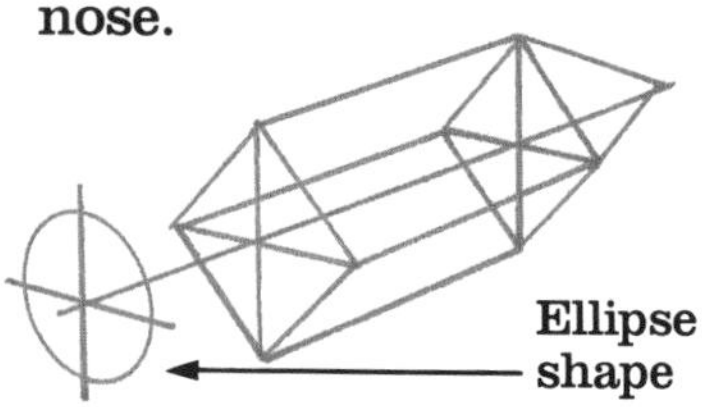

Ellipse shape

Draw the skeleton shape of the station first, starting with the rod and ellipse shape.

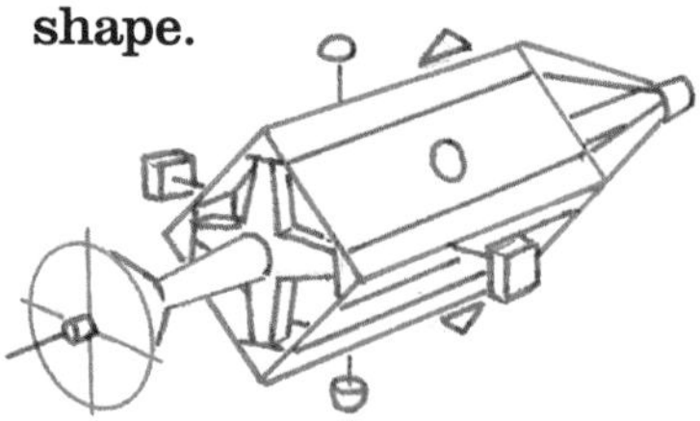

"Whoosh" lines give an idea of movement.

Build up the details, working from the back. As you complete each area, curve the edges of the station, rubbing out rough lines.

E41

Paint thin streaks of white on the surfaces to give a glassy look.

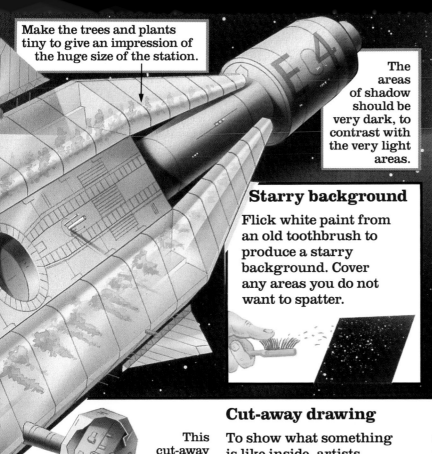

Make the trees and plants tiny to give an impression of the huge size of the station.

The areas of shadow should be very dark, to contrast with the very light areas.

Starry background

Flick white paint from an old toothbrush to produce a starry background. Cover any areas you do not want to spatter.

Enlarging drawings

Draw a grid of equal squares on tracing paper. Place the grid over the drawing.

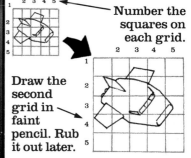

Number the squares on each grid.

Draw the second grid in faint pencil. Rub it out later.

Using a larger sheet of paper, draw a bigger grid with the same number of squares. Copy the drawing square-by-square on to it.*

Cut-away drawing

This cut-away shows a laboratory on the space station.

To show what something is like inside, artists draw a small, "cut-away" section on a drawing. It is a useful technique for showing how a machine works, or the inside of a building. The steps below show you how to use the cut-away technique.

How to draw cut-aways

Draw a rough plan of the inside of the section. (See pages 26-27 for more about plans.)

Draw the main shape of the section and sketch the inside, to get the right perspective.

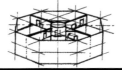

Draw the cut-away area. Rub out any inside details hidden by the walls and go over the part you can see in more detail.

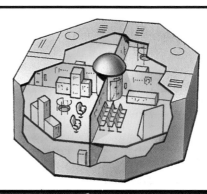

Special effects

Artists often use special techniques to make their drawings look funny or atmospheric. Some of them are shown on these two pages. You can use the colouring styles on any of your drawings.

Cartoons

You can use a bold cartoon technique to make fun drawings, such as the dancing skyscrapers shown here. The buildings have to be recognizable, although the angles are slightly distorted. The details can be sketchy.

Slightly curved edges make buildings look flexible. Add lots of bold movement lines.

You can add a face, or use windows as eyes and a door as a mouth to make buildings look like characters. Chimneys can be drawn as hats, and add ivy for hair.

Use a bold, clear line when drawing the basic shape.

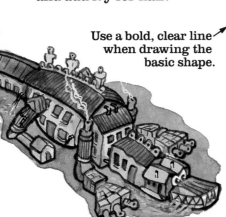

Cartoon technique is often used to make a serious point. In this drawing, a chemical factory has been made into a monster, spouting pollution from its mouth.

Colouring styles

Some artists try to capture the overall atmosphere of a scene rather than emphasize the detail. This is called impressionism. The style is quite loose, although the drawing is still accurate. You can use the techniques shown below to create an impressionist quality.

This technique uses lots ▶ of watery paint. You would need to stretch art paper before beginning. Find out how to do this on page 31.

Pale, washy colours run together to create a misty effect.

Bold, obvious brush strokes give a painting a sense of urgency and excitement. You can also try this with felt tips or coloured pencils.

You could try pastels or coloured pencils for a similar effect.

There is often a great emphasis on the light and shadow of a scene.

You could try using lots of tiny dots of colour. Denser patches of dots can be used for shadows and details such as windows.

Floodlit building

This floodlit building was painted in white and shades of grey over a dark wash.

You could use a white pencil on black paper, instead. After shading, details are added in pen.

A pencil outline of the building will show up on a dark background and act as a guide.

Watery grey is used first, building up to strong, thick white for some details.

The railings are dark as the floodlights are beyond them. This gives the picture depth.

The shadows

As the building is lit from below, the shadows fall in the opposite direction to normal. Anything jutting out will cast a shadow upwards.

Light

Shadows fall upwards.

Drawing and using plans

All buildings start as a set of plans. After an architect has designed the building, plans are worked out and drawn accurately. On these pages you can see how to draw your own plans and use them to make a model.

Technical drawing

The neat, detailed drawing style used for plans is called technical drawing.

Building plans are flat drawings of a 3-D shape. Some of the tools used for technical drawing are shown below.

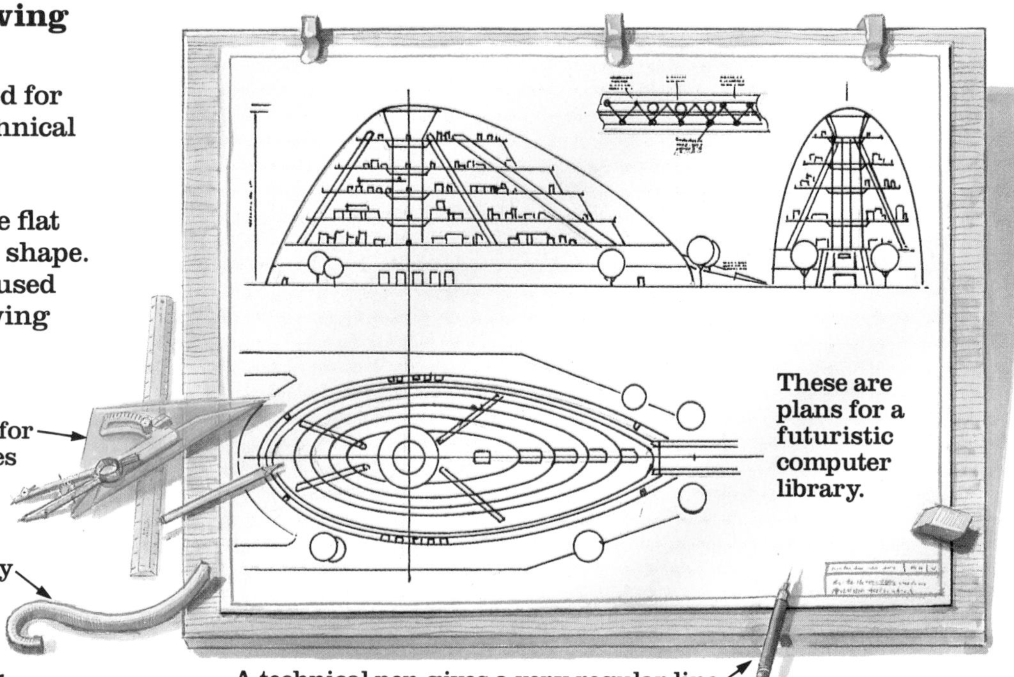

Compasses, set squares and rulers for drawing arcs, angles and straight lines.

A flexi-curve can be adjusted to draw any kind of curve.

These are plans for a futuristic computer library.

A technical pen gives a very regular line.

Drawing plans

There are three main plan-drawing steps.

1. All measurements are worked out and a scale (see below) is set.

2. Information is gathered about all features such as windows, doors, wall thicknesses and even stoves and sinks. Rough plans are then drawn.

3. The finished plan is drawn to scale, using standard symbols for some features. Several elevations (see below) are usually shown.

Scale

A suitable scale is worked out for a plan, depending on the building's size. A scale of 1:100 means that 1cm on the plan represents 1m (or 1:12 is an inch to a foot).

Elevations

Most plans show a building from two or more viewpoints. If the front and the side are shown, for example, these are called the front and side elevations.

Drawing your home

Follow the steps here to make a plan of the inside of your home.

1. First note the length and width of the rooms and corridors of your home. Use a tape measure rather than a ruler.

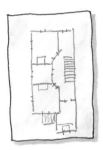

2. Do a rough sketch to help you position everything. Then work out a simple scale to be used on the finished drawing.

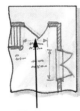

3. Measure windows and doors, noting their positions and direction of opening. Note the number of stairs.

Door opens inwards.

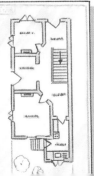

4. Do the final drawing. Add features such as the stove.

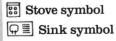
Stove symbol

Sink symbol

Making a model

You could invent your own building and make a model of it. You may find it helpful to draw a scale plan and elevations for it first.

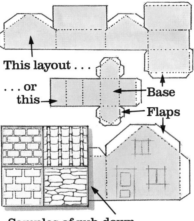

This layout . . .

. . . or this →

Base

Flaps

Samples of rub-down (transfer) details.

Make sure all shadows go in the same direction.

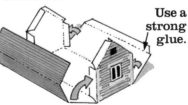

Use a strong glue.

Once you feel confident about drawing plans and making models, you can tackle quite complicated shapes.

Make your drawing of the model on thin cardboard so that it stands up firmly. You will need scissors and glue.

1. Lay out the building in a straight line, or around a base, whichever you prefer. Draw flaps down each open side for glueing together later.

2. Now draw details such as doors, windows and roof tiles. You can buy rub-down (transfer) bricks, stones and tiles if you prefer.

3. Paint or colour your drawing, adding shadows and highlights. You can use paint wash to build up a textured look on walls and roofs.

4. Cut the building out. Fold the flaps and glue the building together. Paint a base on a piece of cardboard and glue your building on to that.

Reconstructions and impressions

Artists are often asked to draw reconstructions of ancient or ruined buildings. The drawings can be used by historians or archaeologists, or as museum displays to show how the buildings looked when they were whole.

Sometimes artists' impressions are done of a building which does not yet exist. The drawings are used for various purposes, such as advertising.

Reconstructing ruins

This is a reconstruction of a Viking settlement. Before drawing anything, the artist studies any plans and photographs, and may visit the site too.

The first sketches are drawn in perspective, using a perspective plan (see bottom of page). You could draw the scene, using the sketch below.

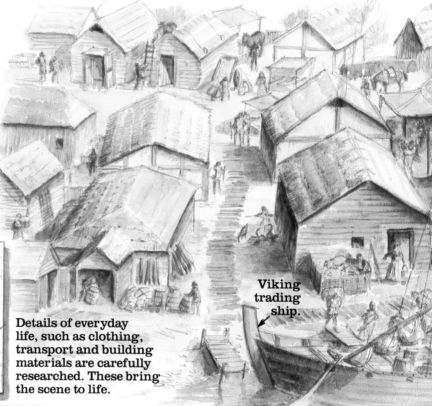

Details of everyday life, such as clothing, transport and building materials are carefully researched. These bring the scene to life.

Viking trading ship.

Making a perspective plan

The artist draws a grid over the original plan and plots each building.* A second grid with an equal number of squares is then drawn in perspective.

Number the squares.

Make this grid bigger if needed.

The positions of the buildings are transferred to the second grid on the corresponding squares. The artist now has a perspective plan. You can try this yourself.

New buildings

This artist's impression of a modern "designer" house has been drawn using architects' plans and a bit of imagination. You can try drawing it yourself.

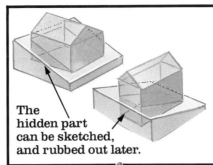

Buildings on slopes

Buildings are always level. On a hill, part of the base of a building is hidden under the ground. Imagine its complete form before drawing a building such as this.

The hidden part can be sketched, and rubbed out later.

Draw the basic block shapes in perspective. The eye level is below the horizon*.

Sketch the hidden corner of the base.→

Dark trees and shadows emphasize corners and add depth.

With impressions, you can choose the angle that the sunlight strikes the building.

Interiors

The insides of buildings can be hard to draw. The scene is close-up, and only part of the whole structure is visible. This means that there are no basic block shapes to build up and the angles are difficult to draw in perspective. This picture shows part of the inside of the house above.

Draw the skeleton shape of the room first. Add the pillars and stairs.

Deep shadows down the edges of the pillars will help them look 3-D. ─

Figures add scale and show how the house will look when in use.

Decide and plot the position of the sun. Draw faint lines from it, to show where light will fall in the house.

Tips and materials

When learning to draw, you need not spend a lot of money on equipment. Choosing the right drawing tools and paper, and learning some basic techniques will help you make a good start.

Choosing drawing tools

The kind of drawing tool you use depends on the style you want. A pen or pencil, for instance, is best for detailed line drawing. A mixture of some of the items below is ideal.

◀ **Pencils** range from very hard to very soft (9H to 7B*). It is best to buy a hard (2H) and a medium (HB) pencil for lines, and a soft (3B) pencil for shading.

Felt or fibre tip pens can be used for ▶ line drawing and colouring. Fibre tips give a thinner line while felt tips are good for large areas of colour.

◀ **Coloured pencils** can give lines of varying thickness and colour strength. They also show up well on coloured paper. Some can double as paints.

Wax crayons, pastels, chalks and ▶ **charcoal** can be blended for a softer look. They are good for large-scale drawings.

◀ **Pens** are widely available, ranging from ballpoints to fine technical drawing pens. They are good for all line drawing.

Watercolour paints can be mixed to ▶ produce a wide range of colours. Buy two paintbrushes – a medium one for general use and a thin one for detail.

Paper

There is a large range of paper available. Most stationery shops sell basic sketch pads, and these are fine for most purposes. The best quality watercolour paper is usually only available from art shops. Do not paint on very thin paper.

Loose-leaf, plain paper is fine for most drawings.——▶

Rougher sketch paper is better for paint.——▶

Rough water-colour paper is ideal for paint, but expensive. ——▶

Airbrushes

If you want to experiment with airbrush technique, a slightly cheaper version, called a modeller's airbrush, is available in art or model shops. They use cans of compressed air instead of costly compressors.

*H stands for hard and B stands for black.

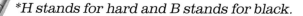

Stretching paper

If you use a lot of paint, it is best to buy sketch or watercolour paper. Stretch paper before beginning, or it will wrinkle when the paint dries.

To stretch paper, you need a board, brown gummed parcel strip, a sponge and water.

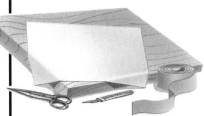

1. Measure and tear off the gummed strips – one length for each side of the paper.

2. Wet (but do not soak) the paper thoroughly under a cold tap with a sponge.

   There should be no pools of water on the paper.

3. Place the paper flat on the board. Working clockwise, tape the edges quickly with dampened gummed strip.

4. Wipe off excess water with a damp sponge. Leave to dry naturally. Do not use while wet.

   Any wrinkles should smooth out when dry.

5. Leave the paper on the board while you paint. Cut it out carefully with a sharp knife when dry.

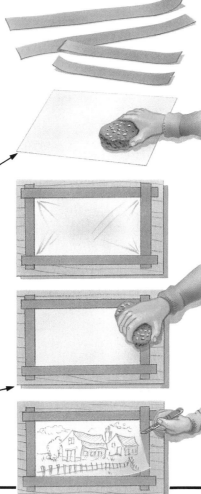

Fixative sprays

Fixative puts a hard, clear finish on a drawing so that it does not fade or smudge. It also allows you to work over a drawing's surface without spoiling existing patterns.

Mouth diffuser

Fixative is available in art shops. You can blow it through a mouth diffuser, or buy a spray can. Avoid breathing the fumes.

Other equipment

Rulers with built-in stencils of shapes or lines can be very useful for your drawings.

Cotton buds can smudge and blend crayons, pastels and chalks.

Plastic erasers rub out pencil lines cleanly. Putty erasers can be twisted to reach tiny areas.

Index

First published in 1991 by Usborne Publishing Ltd,
83-85 Saffron Hill, London EC1N 8RT, England.

Copyright © Usborne Publishing Ltd 1991.

The name Usborne and the device ♈ are trade marks of
Usborne Publishing Ltd.

Printed in Belgium